SHERLOCK HOLMES

in

Silver Blaze

Sir Arthur Conan Doyle

first published in

1892

I am afraid, Watson, that I shall have to go," said Holmes, as we sat down together to our breakfast one morning.

"Go! Where to?"

"To Dartmoor; to King's Pyland."

I was not surprised. Indeed, my only wonder was that he had not already been mixed up in this extraordinary case, which was the one topic of conversation through the length and breadth of England. For a whole day my companion had rambled about the room with his chin upon his chest and his brows knitted, charging and recharging his pipe with the strongest black tobacco, and absolutely deaf to any of my questions or remarks. Fresh editions of every paper had been sent up by our news agent, only to be glanced over and tossed down into a corner. Yet, silent as he was, I knew perfectly well what it was over which he was brooding. There was but one problem before the public which could challenge his powers of analysis, and that was the singular disappearance of the favourite for the Wessex Cup, and the tragic murder of its trainer. When, therefore, he suddenly announced his intention of setting out for the scene of the drama it was only what I had both expected and hoped for.

"I should be most happy to go down with you if I should not be in the way," said I.

"My dear Watson, you would confer a great favour upon me by coming. And I think that your time will not be misspent, for there are points about the case which promise to make it an absolutely unique one. We have, I think, just time to catch our train at Paddington, and I will go further into the matter upon our journey. You would oblige me by bringing with you your very excellent field-glass."

And so it happened that an hour or so later I found myself in the corner of a first-class carriage flying along en route for Exeter, while Sherlock Holmes, with his sharp, eager face framed in his ear-flapped travelling-cap, dipped rapidly into the bundle of fresh papers which he had procured at Paddington. We had left Reading far behind us before he thrust the last one of them under the seat, and offered me his cigar-case.

"We are going well," said he, looking out the window and glancing at his watch. "Our rate at present is fifty-three and a half miles an hour."

"I have not observed the quarter-mile posts," said I.

"Nor have I. But

the telegraph posts upon this line are sixty yards apart, and the calculation is a simple one. I presume that you have looked into this matter of the murder of John Straker and the disappearance of Silver Blaze?"

"I have seen what the Telegraph and the Chronicle have to say."

"It is one of those cases where the art of the reasoner should be used rather for the sifting of details than for the acquiring of fresh evidence. The tragedy has been so uncommon, so complete and of such personal importance to so many people, that we are suffering from a plethora of surmise, conjecture, and hypothesis. The difficulty is to detach the framework of fact—of absolute undeniable fact—from the embellishments of theorists and reporters. Then, having established ourselves upon this sound basis, it is our duty to see what inferences may be drawn and what are the special points upon which the whole mystery turns. On Tuesday evening I received telegrams from both Colonel Ross, the owner of the horse, and from Inspector Gregory, who is looking after the case, inviting my co-operation."

"Tuesday evening!" I exclaimed. "And this is Thursday morning. Why didn't you go down yesterday?"

"Because I made a blunder, my dear Watson—which is, I am afraid, a more common occurrence than any one would think who only knew me through your memoirs. The fact is that I could not believe it possible that the most remarkable horse in England could long remain concealed, especially in so sparsely inhabited a place as the north of Dartmoor. From hour to hour yesterday I expected to hear that he had been found, and that his abductor was the murderer of John Straker. When, however, another morning had come, and I found that beyond the arrest of young Fitzroy Simpson nothing had been done, I felt that it was time for me to take action. Yet in some ways I feel that yesterday has not been wasted."

"You have formed a theory, then?"

"At least I have got a grip of the essential facts of the case. I shall enumerate them to you, for nothing clears up a case so much as stating it to another person, and I can hardly expect your co-operation if I do not show you the position from which we start."

I lay back against the cushions, puffing at my cigar, while Holmes, leaning forward, with his long, thin forefinger checking off the points upon the palm of his left hand, gave me a sketch of the events which had led to our journey.

"Silver Blaze," said he, "is from the Isonomy stock, and holds as brilliant a record as his famous ancestor. He is now in his fifth year, and has brought in turn each of the prizes of the turf to Colonel Ross,

his fortunate owner.
Up to the time of the
catastrophe he was
the first favourite
for the Wessex Cup,
the betting being
three to one on
him. He has always,
however, been a
prime favourite with
the racing public,
and has never yet
disappointed them,
so that even at those
odds enormous sums
of money have been

laid upon him. It is obvious, therefore, that there were many people who had the strongest interest in preventing Silver Blaze from being there at the fall of the flag next Tuesday.

"The fact was, of course, appreciated at King's Pyland, where the Colonel's training-stable is situated. Every precaution was taken to guard the favourite. The trainer, John Straker, is a retired jockey who rode in Colonel Ross's colours before he became too heavy for the weighing-chair. He has served the Colonel for five years as jockey and for seven as trainer, and has always shown himself to be a zealous and honest servant. Under him were three lads; for the establishment was a small one, containing only four horses in all. One of these lads sat up each night in the stable, while the others slept in the loft. All three bore excellent characters. John Straker, who is a married man, lived in a small villa about two hundred yards from the stables. He has no children, keeps one maid-servant, and is comfortably off. The country round is very lonely, but about half a mile to the north there is a small cluster of villas which have been built by a Tavistock contractor for the use of invalids and others who may wish to enjoy the pure Dartmoor air. Tavistock itself lies two miles to the west, while across the moor, also about two miles distant, is the larger training establishment of Mapleton, which belongs to Lord Backwater, and is managed by Silas Brown. In every other direction the moor is a complete wilderness, inhabited only by a few roaming gypsies. Such was the general situation last Monday night when the catastrophe occurred.

"On that evening the horses had been exercised and watered as usual, and the stables were locked up at nine o'clock. Two of the lads walked up to the trainer's house, where they had supper in the kitchen, while the third, Ned Hunter, remained on guard. At a few minutes after nine the maid, Edith Baxter, carried down to the stables his supper, which consisted of a dish of curried mutton. She took no liquid, as there was a water-tap in the stables, and it was the rule that the lad on duty should drink nothing else. The maid carried a lantern with her, as it was very dark and the path ran across the open moor.

"Edith Baxter was within thirty yards of the stables, when a man appeared out of the darkness and called to her to stop.

As he stepped into the circle of yellow light thrown by the lantern she saw that he was a person of gentlemanly bearing, dressed in a grey suit of tweeds, with a cloth cap. He wore gaiters, and carried a heavy stick with a knob to it. She was most impressed, however, by the extreme pallor of his face and by the nervousness of his manner. His age, she thought, would be rather over thirty than under it.

"'Can you tell me where I am?' he asked. 'I had almost made up my mind to sleep on the moor, when I saw the light of your lantern.'

"'You are close to the King's Pyland training-stables,' said she.

"'Oh, indeed! What a stroke of luck!' he cried. 'I understand that a stable-boy sleeps there alone every night. Perhaps that is his supper which you are carrying to him. Now I am sure that you would not be too proud to earn the price of a new dress, would you?'

He took a piece of white paper folded up out of his waistcoat pocket. 'See that the boy has this to-night, and you shall have the prettiest frock that money can buy.'

"She was frightened by the earnestness of his manner, and ran past him to the window through which she was accustomed to hand the meals. It was already opened, and Hunter was seated at the small table inside. She had begun to tell him of what had happened, when the stranger came up again.

"'Good-evening,' said he, looking through the window. 'I wanted to have a word with you.' The girl has sworn that as he spoke she noticed the corner of the little paper packet protruding from his closed hand.

"'What business have you here?' asked the lad.

"'It's business that may put something into your pocket,' said the other. 'You've two horses in for the Wessex Cup—Silver Blaze and

Bayard. Let me have the straight tip and you won't be a loser. Is it a fact that at the weights Bayard could give the other a hundred yards in five furlongs, and that the stable have put their money on him?'

"'So, you're one of those damned touts!' cried the lad. 'I'll show you how we serve them in King's Pyland.' He sprang up and rushed across the stable to unloose the dog. The girl fled away to the house, but as she ran she looked back and saw that the stranger was leaning through the window. A minute later, however, when Hunter rushed out with the hound he was gone, and though he ran all round the buildings he failed to find any trace of him."

"One moment," I asked. "Did the stable-boy, when he ran out with the dog, leave the door unlocked behind him?"

"Excellent, Watson, excellent!" murmured my companion. "The importance of the point struck me so forcibly that I sent a special wire to Dartmoor yesterday to clear the matter up. The boy locked the door before he left it. The window, I may add, was not large enough for a man to get through.

"Hunter waited until his fellow-grooms had returned, when he sent a message to the trainer and told him what had occurred. Straker was excited at hearing the account, although he does not seem to have quite realized its true significance. It left him, however, vaguely uneasy, and Mrs. Straker, waking at one in the morning, found that he was dressing. In reply to her inquiries, he said that he could not sleep on account of his anxiety about the horses, and that he intended to walk down to the stables to see that all was well. She begged him to remain at home, as she could hear the rain pattering against the window, but in spite of her entreaties he pulled on his large mackintosh and left the house.

"Mrs. Straker awoke at seven in the morning, to find that her husband had not yet returned. She dressed herself hastily, called the maid, and set off for the stables. The door was open; inside, huddled together upon a chair, Hunter was sunk in a state of absolute stupor, the favourite's stall was empty, and there were no signs of his trainer.

"The two lads who slept in the chaff-cutting loft above the harness-room were quickly aroused. They had heard nothing during the night, for they are both sound sleepers. Hunter was obviously under the influence of some powerful drug, and as no sense could be got out of him, he was left to sleep it off while the two lads and the two women ran out in search of the absentees. They still had hopes that the trainer had for some reason taken out the horse for early exercise, but on ascending the knoll near the house, from which all the neighbouring moors were visible, they not only could see no signs of the missing favourite, but they perceived something which warned them that they were in the presence of a tragedy.

"About a quarter of a mile from the stables John Straker's overcoat was flapping from a furze-bush. Immediately beyond there was a bowl-shaped depression in the moor, and at the bottom of this was found the dead body of the unfortunate trainer. His head had been shattered by a savage blow from some heavy weapon, and he was wounded on the thigh, where there was a long, clean cut, inflicted evidently by some very sharp instrument. It was clear, however, that Straker had defended himself vigorously against his assailants, for in his right hand he held a small knife, which was clotted with blood up to the handle, while in his left he clasped a red and black silk cravat, which was recognised by the maid as having been worn on the preceding evening by the stranger who had visited the stables.

"Hunter, on recovering from his stupor, was also quite positive as to the ownership of the cravat. He was equally certain that the same stranger had, while standing at the window, drugged his curried mutton, and so deprived the stables of their watchman.

"As to the missing horse, there were abundant proofs in the mud which lay at the bottom of the fatal hollow that he had been there at the time of the struggle. But from that morning he has disappeared, and although a large reward has been offered, and all the gypsies of Dartmoor are on the alert, no news has come of him. Finally, an analysis has shown that the remains of his supper left by the stable-lad contain an appreciable quantity of powdered opium, while the people at the house partook of the same dish on the same night without any ill effect.

"Those are the main facts of the case, stripped of all surmise, and stated as baldly as possible. I shall now recapitulate what the police have done in the matter.

"Inspector Gregory, to whom the case has been committed, is an extremely competent officer. Were he but gifted with imagination he might rise to great heights in his profession. On his arrival he promptly found and arrested the man upon whom suspicion naturally rested. There was little difficulty in finding him, for he inhabited one of those villas which I have mentioned. His name, it appears, was Fitzroy Simpson.

He was a man of excellent birth and education, who had squandered a fortune upon the turf, and who lived now by doing a little quiet and genteel book-making in the sporting clubs of London. An examination of his betting-book shows that bets to the amount of five thousand pounds had been registered by him against the favourite.

"On being arrested he volunteered the statement that he had come down to Dartmoor in the hope of getting some information about the King's Pyland horses, and also about Desborough, the second favourite, which was in charge of Silas Brown at the Mapleton stables. He did not attempt to deny that he had acted as described upon the evening before, but declared that he had no sinister designs, and had simply wished to obtain first-hand information. When confronted with his cravat, he turned very pale, and was utterly unable to account for its presence in the hand of the murdered man. His wet clothing showed that he had been out in the storm of the night before, and his stick, which was a Penang-lawyer weighted with lead, was just such a weapon as might, by repeated blows, have inflicted the terrible injuries to which the trainer had succumbed.

"On the other hand, there was no wound upon his person, while the state of Straker's knife would show that one at least of his assailants must bear his mark upon him. There you have it all in a nutshell, Watson, and if you can give me any light I shall be infinitely obliged to you."

I had listened with the greatest interest to the statement which Holmes, with characteristic clearness, had laid before me. Though most of the facts were familiar to me, I had not sufficiently appreciated their relative importance, nor their connection to each other.

"Is it not possible," I suggested, "that the incised wound upon Straker may have been caused by his own knife in the convulsive struggles which follow any brain injury?"

"It is more than possible; it is probable," said Holmes. "In that case one of the main points in favour of the accused disappears."

"And yet," said I, "even now I fail to understand what the theory of the police can be."

"I am afraid that whatever theory we state has very grave objections to it," returned my companion. "The police imagine, I take it, that this

Fitzroy Simpson, having drugged the lad, and having in some way obtained a duplicate key, opened the stable door and took out the horse, with the intention, apparently, of kidnapping him altogether. His bridle is missing, so that Simpson must have put this on. Then, having left the door open behind him, he was leading the horse away over the moor, when he was either met or overtaken by the trainer. A row naturally ensued. Simpson beat out the trainer's brains with his heavy stick without receiving any injury from the small knife which Straker used in self-defence, and then the thief either led the horse on to some secret hiding-place, or else it may have bolted during the struggle, and be now wandering out on the moors. That is the case as it appears to the police, and improbable as it is, all other explanations are more improbable still. However, I shall very quickly test the matter when I am once upon the spot, and until then

I cannot really see how we can get much further than our present position."

It was evening before we reached the little town of Tavistock, which lies, like the boss of a shield, in the middle of the huge circle of Dartmoor. Two gentlemen were awaiting us in the station—the one a tall, fair man with lion-like hair and beard and curiously penetrating light blue eyes; the other a small, alert person, very neat and dapper, in a frock-coat and gaiters, with trim little side-whiskers and an eye-glass. The latter was Colonel Ross, the well-known sportsman; the other, Inspector Gregory, a man who was rapidly making his name in the English detective service.

"I am delighted that you have come down, Mr. Holmes," said the Colonel. "The Inspector here has done all that could possibly be suggested, but I wish to leave no stone unturned in trying to avenge poor Straker and in recovering my horse."

"Have there been any fresh developments?" asked Holmes.

"I am sorry to say that we have made very little progress," said the Inspector. "We have an open carriage outside, and as you would no doubt like to see the place before the light fails, we might talk it over as we drive."

A minute later we were all seated in a comfortable landau, and were rattling through the quaint old Devonshire city. Inspector Gregory was full of his case, and poured out a stream of remarks, while Holmes threw in an occasional question or interjection. Colonel Ross leaned back with his arms folded and his hat tilted over his eyes, while I listened with interest to the dialogue of the two detectives. Gregory was formulating his theory, which was almost exactly what Holmes had foretold in the train.

"The net is drawn

pretty close round Fitzroy Simpson," he remarked, "and I believe myself that he is our man. At the same time I recognise that the evidence is purely circumstantial, and that some new development may upset it."

"How about Straker's knife?"

"We have quite come to the conclusion

that he wounded himself in his fall."

"My friend Dr. Watson made that suggestion to me as we came down. If so, it would tell against this man Simpson."

"Undoubtedly. He has neither a knife nor any sign of a wound. The evidence against him is certainly very strong. He had a great interest in the disappearance of the favourite. He lies under suspicion of having poisoned the stable-boy, he was undoubtedly out in the storm, he was armed with a heavy stick, and his cravat was found in the dead man's hand. I really think we have enough to go before a jury."

Holmes shook his

head. "A clever counsel would tear it all to rags," said he. "Why should he take the horse out of the stable? If he wished to injure it why could he not do it there? Has a duplicate key been found in his possession? What chemist sold him the powdered opium? Above all, where could he, a stranger to the district, hide a horse, and such a horse as this? What is his own explanation as to the paper which he wished the maid to give to the stable-boy?"

"He says that it was a ten-pound note. One was found in his purse. But your other difficulties are not so formidable as they seem. He is not a stranger to the district. He has twice lodged at Tavistock in the summer. The opium was probably brought from London. The key, having served its purpose, would be hurled away. The horse may be at the bottom of one of the pits or old mines upon the moor."

"What does he say

about the cravat?"

"He acknowledges that it is his, and declares that he had lost it. But a new element has been introduced into the case which may account for his leading the horse from the stable."

Holmes pricked up his ears.

"We have found

traces which show that a party of gypsies encamped on Monday night within a mile of the spot where the murder took place. On Tuesday they were gone. Now, presuming that there was some understanding between Simpson and these gypsies, might he not have been leading the horse to them when he was overtaken, and may they not have him now?"

"It is certainly possible."

"The moor is being scoured for these gypsies. I have also examined every stable and out-house in Tavistock, and for a radius of ten miles."

"There is another

training-stable quite close, I understand?"

"Yes, and that is a factor which we must certainly not neglect. As Desborough, their horse, was second in the betting, they had an interest in the disappearance of the favourite. Silas Brown, the trainer, is known to have had large bets upon the event, and he was no friend to poor Straker. We have, however, examined the stables, and there is nothing to connect him with the affair."

"And nothing to connect this man Simpson with the interests of the Mapleton stables?"

"Nothing at all."

Holmes leaned back

in the carriage, and the conversation ceased. A few minutes later our driver pulled up at a neat little red-brick villa with overhanging eaves which stood by the road. Some distance off, across a paddock, lay a long grey-tiled out-building. In every other direction the low curves of the moor, bronze-coloured from the fading ferns, stretched away to the sky-line, broken only by the steeples of Tavistock, and by a cluster of houses away to the westward which marked the Mapleton stables. We all sprang out with the exception of Holmes, who continued to lean back with his eyes fixed upon the sky in front of him, entirely absorbed in his own thoughts. It was only when I touched his arm that he roused himself with a violent start and stepped out of the carriage.

"Excuse me," said he, turning to Colonel Ross, who had looked at him in some surprise. "I was day-dreaming." There was a gleam in his eyes and a suppressed excitement in his manner which convinced me, used as I was to his ways, that his hand was upon a clue, though I could not imagine where he had found it.

"Perhaps you would prefer at once to go on to the scene of the crime, Mr.

Holmes?" said Gregory.

"I think that I should prefer to stay here a little and go into one or two questions of detail. Straker was brought back here, I presume?"

"Yes; he lies upstairs. The inquest is to-morrow."

"He has been in your service some years,

Colonel Ross?"

"I have always found him an excellent servant."

"I presume that you made an inventory of what he had in his pockets at the time of his death, Inspector?"

"I have the things themselves in the sitting-room, if you would care to see them."

"I should be very glad." We all filed into the front room and sat round the central table while the Inspector unlocked a square tin box and laid a small heap of things before us. There was a box of vestas, two inches of tallow candle, an A.D.P. briar-root pipe, a pouch of seal-skin with half an ounce of long-cut Cavendish, a silver watch with a gold chain, five sovereigns in gold, an aluminium pencil-case, a few papers, and an ivory-handled knife with a very delicate, inflexible blade marked Weiss & Co., London.

"This is a very singular knife," said Holmes, lifting it

up and examining it minutely. "I presume, as I see blood-stains upon it, that it is the one which was found in the dead man's grasp. Watson, this knife is surely in your line?"

"It is what we call a cataract knife," said I.

"I thought so. A very delicate blade devised for very

delicate work. A strange thing for a man to carry with him upon a rough expedition, especially as it would not shut in his pocket."

"The tip was guarded by a disk of cork which we found beside his body," said the Inspector. "His wife tells us that the knife had lain upon the dressing-table, and that he had picked it up as he left the room. It was a poor weapon, but perhaps the best that he could lay his hands on at the moment."

"Very possible. How about these papers?"

"Three of them are receipted hay-dealers' accounts. One of them is a letter of instructions from Colonel Ross. This other is a milliner's account for thirty-seven pounds fifteen made out by Madame Lesurier, of Bond Street, to William Derbyshire. Mrs. Straker tells us that Derbyshire was a friend of her husband's and that occasionally his letters were addressed here."

"Madam Derbyshire had somewhat expensive tastes," remarked Holmes, glancing down the account. "Twenty-two guineas is rather heavy for a single costume. However there appears to be nothing more to learn, and we may now go down to the scene of the crime."

As we emerged from the sitting-room a woman, who had been waiting in the passage, took a step forward and laid her hand upon the Inspector's sleeve. Her face was haggard and thin and eager, stamped with the print of a recent horror.

"Have you got them? Have you found

them?" she panted.

"No, Mrs. Straker. But Mr. Holmes here has come from London to help us, and we shall do all that is possible."

"Surely I met you in Plymouth at a garden-party some little time ago, Mrs. Straker?" said Holmes.

"No, sir; you are

mistaken."

"Dear me! Why, I could have sworn to it. You wore a costume of dove-coloured silk with ostrich-feather trimming."

"I never had such a dress, sir," answered the lady.

"Ah, that quite settles it," said Holmes. And with an

apology he followed the Inspector outside. A short walk across the moor took us to the hollow in which the body had been found. At the brink of it was the furze-bush upon which the coat had been hung.

"There was no wind that night, I understand," said Holmes.

"None; but very

heavy rain."

"In that case the overcoat was not blown against the furze-bush, but placed there."

"Yes, it was laid across the bush."

"You fill me with interest, I perceive that the ground has been trampled up a good deal. No doubt many feet have been here since Monday night."

"A piece of matting has been laid here at the side, and we have all stood upon that."

"Excellent."

"In this bag I have one of the boots which Straker wore, one of Fitzroy Simpson's shoes, and a cast horseshoe of

Silver Blaze."

"My dear Inspector, you surpass yourself!" Holmes took the bag, and, descending into the hollow, he pushed the matting into a more central position. Then stretching himself upon his face and leaning his chin upon his hands, he made a careful study of the trampled mud in front of him. "Hullo!" said he, suddenly. "What's this?" It was a wax vesta half burned, which was so coated with mud that it looked at first like a little chip of wood.

"I cannot think how I came to overlook it," said the Inspector, with an expression of annoyance.

"It was invisible, buried in the mud. I

only saw it because I was looking for it."

"What! You expected to find it?"

"I thought it not unlikely."

He took the boots from the bag, and compared the impressions of each of them with marks upon the ground. Then he clambered up to the rim of the hollow, and crawled about among the ferns and bushes.

"I am afraid that there are no more tracks," said the Inspector. "I have examined the ground very carefully for a hundred yards in each direction."

"Indeed!" said Holmes, rising. "I should not have the impertinence to do it again after what you say. But I should like to take a little walk over the moor before it grows dark, that I may know my ground to-morrow, and I think that I shall put this horseshoe into my pocket for luck."

Colonel Ross, who had shown some signs of impatience at my companion's quiet and systematic

method of work,
glanced at his watch.
"I wish you would
come back with me,
Inspector," said he.
"There are several
points on which I
should like your
advice, and especially
as to whether we
do not owe it to the
public to remove our
horse's name from
the entries for the
Cup."

"Certainly not," cried Holmes, with decision. "I should let the name stand."

The Colonel bowed. "I am very glad to have had your opinion, sir," said he. "You will find us at poor Straker's house when you have finished your walk, and we can drive together into Tavistock."

He turned back with

the Inspector, while
Holmes and I walked
slowly across the
moor. The sun was
beginning to sink
behind the stables
of Mapleton, and the
long, sloping plain
in front of us was
tinged with gold,
deepening into rich,
ruddy browns where
the faded ferns and
brambles caught
the evening light.
But the glories of

the landscape were all wasted upon my companion, who was sunk in the deepest thought.

"It's this way, Watson," said he at last. "We may leave the question of who killed John Straker for the instant, and confine ourselves to finding out what has become of the horse. Now, supposing that he broke away during or after the tragedy, where could he have gone to? The horse is a very gregarious creature. If left to himself his instincts would have been either to return to King's Pyland or go over to Mapleton. Why should he run wild upon the moor? He would surely have been seen by now. And why should gypsies kidnap him? These people always clear out when they hear of trouble, for they do not wish to be pestered by the police. They could not hope to sell such a horse. They would run a great risk and gain nothing by taking him. Surely that is clear."

"Where is he, then?"

"I have already said

that he must have
gone to King's Pyland
or to Mapleton.
He is not at King's
Pyland. Therefore
he is at Mapleton.
Let us take that as a
working hypothesis
and see what it leads
us to. This part of
the moor, as the
Inspector remarked,
is very hard and dry.
But it falls away
towards Mapleton,
and you can see from

here that there is a long hollow over yonder, which must have been very wet on Monday night. If our supposition is correct, then the horse must have crossed that, and there is the point where we should look for his tracks."

We had been walking briskly during this conversation, and a

few more minutes brought us to the hollow in question. At Holmes' request I walked down the bank to the right, and he to the left, but I had not taken fifty paces before I heard him give a shout, and saw him waving his hand to me. The track of a horse was plainly outlined in the soft earth in front of him, and the shoe which he took from his pocket exactly fitted the impression.

"See the value of imagination," said Holmes. "It is the one quality which Gregory lacks. We imagined what might have happened, acted upon the supposition, and find ourselves justified. Let us proceed."

We crossed the

marshy bottom
and passed over a
quarter of a mile of
dry, hard turf. Again
the ground sloped,
and again we came
on the tracks. Then
we lost them for half
a mile, but only to
pick them up once
more quite close
to Mapleton. It was
Holmes who saw
them first, and he
stood pointing with a
look of triumph upon

his face. A man's track was visible beside the horse's.

"The horse was alone before," I cried.

"Quite so. It was alone before. Hullo, what is this?"

The double track turned sharp off and took the direction of King's Pyland. Holmes whistled, and we both followed along after it. His eyes were on the trail, but I happened to look a little to one side, and saw to my surprise the same tracks coming back again in the opposite direction.

"One for you, Watson," said Holmes, when I pointed it out. "You have saved us a long walk, which would have brought us back on our own traces. Let us follow the return track."

We had not to go far. It ended at the paving of asphalt which led up to the gates of the Mapleton stables. As we approached, a groom ran out from them.

"We don't want any loiterers about here,"

said he.

"I only wished to ask a question," said Holmes, with his finger and thumb in his waistcoat pocket. "Should I be too early to see your master, Mr. Silas Brown, if I were to call at five o'clock to-morrow morning?"

"Bless you, sir, if any one is about he will be, for he is always the first stirring. But here he is, sir, to answer your questions for himself. No, sir, no; it is as much as my place is worth to let him see me touch your money. Afterwards, if you like."

As Sherlock Holmes replaced the half-crown which he had drawn from his pocket, a fierce-looking elderly man strode out from the gate with a hunting-crop swinging in his hand.

"What's this, Dawson!" he cried. "No gossiping! Go about your business! And you, what the devil do you want here?"

"Ten minutes' talk with you, my good sir," said Holmes

in the sweetest of voices.

"I've no time to talk to every gadabout. We want no strangers here. Be off, or you may find a dog at your heels."

Holmes leaned forward and whispered something in the trainer's ear. He started violently and flushed to the temples.

"It's a lie!" he shouted, "an infernal lie!"

"Very good. Shall we argue about it here in public or talk it over in your parlour?"

"Oh, come in if you wish to."

Holmes smiled. "I shall not keep you more than a few minutes, Watson," said he. "Now, Mr.

Brown, I am quite at your disposal."

It was twenty minutes, and the reds had all faded into greys before Holmes and the trainer reappeared. Never have I seen such a change as had been brought about in Silas Brown in that short time. His face was ashy pale, beads of perspiration shone upon his brow, and his hands shook until the hunting-crop wagged like a branch in the wind. His bullying, overbearing manner was all gone too, and he cringed along at my companion's side like a dog with its master.

"Your instructions will be done. It shall all be done," said he.

"There must be

no mistake," said Holmes, looking round at him. The other winced as he read the menace in his eyes.

"Oh no, there shall be no mistake. It shall be there. Should I change it first or not?"

Holmes thought a little and then burst out laughing. "No, don't," said he; "I shall write to you about it. No tricks, now, or—"

"Oh, you can trust me, you can trust me!"

"Yes, I think I can. Well, you shall hear from me to-morrow." He turned upon his heel, disregarding the trembling hand which the other held out to him, and we set off for King's Pyland.

"A more perfect compound of the bully, coward, and sneak than Master Silas Brown I have seldom met with," remarked Holmes as we trudged along together.

"He has the horse, then?"

"He tried to bluster out of it, but I described to him so exactly what his actions had been upon that morning that he is convinced that I was watching him. Of course you observed the peculiarly square toes in the impressions, and that his own boots exactly corresponded to them. Again, of course no subordinate would have dared to do such a thing. I described to him how, when according to his custom he was the first down, he perceived a strange horse wandering over the moor. How he went out to it, and his astonishment at recognising, from the white forehead which has given the favourite its name, that chance had put in his power the only horse which could beat the one upon which he had put his money. Then I described how his first impulse had been to lead him back to King's Pyland, and how the devil had shown him how he could hide the horse until the race was over, and how he had led it back and concealed it at Mapleton. When I told him every detail he gave it up and thought only of saving his own skin."

"But his stables had been searched?"

"Oh, an old horse-faker like him has many a dodge."

"But are you not afraid to leave the horse in his power now, since he has every interest in injuring it?"

"My dear fellow, he will guard it as the apple of his eye. He knows that his only hope of mercy is to produce it safe."

"Colonel Ross did not impress me as a man who would be likely to show much mercy in any case."

"The matter does not rest with Colonel Ross. I follow my own methods, and tell as much or as little as I choose. That is the advantage of being unofficial. I don't know whether you observed it, Watson, but the Colonel's manner has been just a trifle cavalier to me. I am inclined now to have a little amusement at his expense. Say nothing to him about the horse."

"Certainly not without your permission."

"And of course this is all quite a minor point compared to the question of who killed John Straker."

"And you will devote yourself to that?"

"On the contrary, we both go back to London by the night train."

I was thunderstruck by my friend's words. We had only been a few hours in Devonshire, and that he should give up an investigation which he had begun so brilliantly was quite incomprehensible to me. Not a word more could I draw from him until we were back at the trainer's house. The Colonel and the Inspector were awaiting us in the parlour.

"My friend and I return to town by the night-express," said Holmes. "We have had a charming little breath of your beautiful Dartmoor air."

The Inspector opened his eyes, and the Colonel's lip curled in a sneer.

"So you despair of arresting the murderer of poor Straker," said he.

Holmes shrugged his shoulders. "There are certainly grave difficulties in the way," said he. "I have every hope, however, that your horse will start upon Tuesday, and I beg that you will have your jockey in readiness. Might I

ask for a photograph
of Mr. John Straker?"

The Inspector took
one from an envelope
and handed it to him.

"My dear Gregory,
you anticipate all my
wants. If I might ask
you to wait here for
an instant, I have
a question which I
should like to put to
the maid."

"I must say that I am

rather disappointed in our London consultant," said Colonel Ross, bluntly, as my friend left the room. "I do not see that we are any further than when he came."

"At least you have his assurance that your horse will run," said I.

"Yes, I have his assurance," said the

Colonel, with a shrug of his shoulders. "I should prefer to have the horse."

I was about to make some reply in defence of my friend when he entered the room again.

"Now, gentlemen," said he, "I am quite ready for Tavistock."

As we stepped into the carriage one of

the stable-lads held the door open for us. A sudden idea seemed to occur to Holmes, for he leaned forward and touched the lad upon the sleeve.

"You have a few sheep in the paddock," he said. "Who attends to them?"

"I do, sir."

"Have you noticed anything amiss with them of late?"

"Well, sir, not of much account; but three of them have gone lame, sir."

I could see that Holmes was extremely pleased, for he chuckled and rubbed his hands together.

"A long shot,

Watson; a very long shot," said he, pinching my arm. "Gregory, let me recommend to your attention this singular epidemic among the sheep. Drive on, coachman!"

Colonel Ross still wore an expression which showed the poor opinion which he had formed of my companion's ability, but I saw by the Inspector's face that his attention had been keenly aroused.

"You consider that to be important?" he asked.

"Exceedingly so."

"Is there any point to which you would wish to draw my attention?"

"To the curious

incident of the dog in the night-time."

"The dog did nothing in the night-time."

"That was the curious incident," remarked Sherlock Holmes.

Four days later Holmes and I were again in the train, bound for Winchester to see the race for the Wessex Cup.

Colonel Ross met us by appointment outside the station, and we drove in his drag to the course beyond the town. His face was grave, and his manner was cold in the extreme.

"I have seen nothing of my horse," said he.

"I suppose that you would know him when you saw him?" asked

Holmes.

The Colonel was very angry. "I have been on the turf for twenty years, and never was asked such a question as that before," said he. "A child would know Silver Blaze, with his white forehead and his mottled off-foreleg."

"How is the betting?"

"Well, that is the curious part of it. You could have got fifteen to one yesterday, but the price has become shorter and shorter, until you can hardly get three to one now."

"Hum!" said Holmes. "Somebody knows something, that is clear."

As the drag drew

up in the enclosure near the grand stand I glanced at the card to see the entries. It ran:—

Wessex Plate. 50 sovs each h ft with 1000 sovs added for four and five year olds. Second, £300. Third, £200. New course (one mile and five furlongs).

1. Mr. Heath Newton's The Negro (red cap,

cinnamon jacket).

2. Colonel Wardlaw's Pugilist (pink cap, blue and black jacket).

3. Lord Backwater's Desborough (yellow cap and sleeves).

4. Colonel Ross's Silver Blaze (black cap, red jacket).

5. Duke of Balmoral's Iris (yellow and black

stripes).

6. Lord Singleford's Rasper (purple cap, black sleeves).

"We scratched our other one, and put all hopes on your word," said the Colonel. "Why, what is that? Silver Blaze favourite?"

"Five to four against

Silver Blaze!" roared the ring. "Five to four against Silver Blaze! Five to fifteen against Desborough! Five to four on the field!"

"There are the numbers up," I cried. "They are all six there."

"All six there? Then my horse is running," cried the Colonel in great agitation. "But

I don't see him. My colours have not passed."

"Only five have passed. This must be he."

As I spoke a powerful bay horse swept out from the weighing enclosure and cantered past us, bearing on its back the well-known black and red of the Colonel.

"That's not my horse," cried the owner. "That beast has not a white hair upon its body. What is this that you have done, Mr. Holmes?"

"Well, well, let us see how he gets on," said my friend, imperturbably. For a few minutes he gazed through my field-glass. "Capital! An excellent start!"

he cried suddenly. "There they are, coming round the curve!"

From our drag we had a superb view as they came up the straight. The six horses were so close together that a carpet could have covered them, but half way up the yellow of the Mapleton stable showed to the front. Before they reached us, however, Desborough's bolt was shot, and the Colonel's horse, coming away with a rush, passed the post a good six lengths before its rival, the Duke of Balmoral's Iris making a bad third.

"It's my race, anyhow," gasped the

Colonel, passing his hand over his eyes. "I confess that I can make neither head nor tail of it. Don't you think that you have kept up your mystery long enough, Mr. Holmes?"

"Certainly, Colonel, you shall know everything. Let us all go round and have a look at the horse together. Here he is," he continued, as we made our way into the weighing enclosure, where only owners and their friends find admittance. "You have only to wash his face and his leg in spirits of wine, and you will find that he is the same old Silver Blaze as ever."

"You take my breath away!"

"I found him in the hands of a faker, and took the liberty of running him just as he was sent over."

"My dear sir, you have done wonders. The horse looks very fit and well. It never went better in its life. I owe you a thousand apologies for having doubted your ability. You have done me a great service by recovering my horse. You would do me a greater still if you could lay your hands on the murderer of John Straker."

"I have done so," said Holmes quietly.

The Colonel and I stared at him in amazement. "You have got him! Where is he, then?"

"He is here."

"Here! Where?"

"In my company at the present moment."

The Colonel flushed angrily. "I quite recognise that I am under obligations to you, Mr. Holmes," said he, "but I must regard what you have just said as either a very bad joke or an insult."

Sherlock Holmes laughed. "I assure you that I have not associated you with the crime, Colonel," said he. "The real murderer is standing immediately behind you." He stepped past and laid his hand upon the glossy neck of the thoroughbred.

"The horse!" cried both the Colonel and

myself.

"Yes, the horse. And it may lessen his guilt if I say that it was done in self-defence, and that John Straker was a man who was entirely unworthy of your confidence. But there goes the bell, and as I stand to win a little on this next race, I shall defer a lengthy explanation until a more fitting time."

We had the corner
of a Pullman car
to ourselves that
evening as we
whirled back to
London, and I fancy
that the journey
was a short one
to Colonel Ross as
well as to myself,
as we listened to
our companion's
narrative of the
events which had

occurred at the Dartmoor training-stables upon the Monday night, and the means by which he had unravelled them.

"I confess," said he, "that any theories which I had formed from the newspaper reports were entirely erroneous. And yet there were indications there, had they not been overlaid by other details which concealed their true import. I went to Devonshire with the conviction that Fitzroy Simpson was the true culprit, although, of course, I saw that the evidence against him was by no means complete. It was while I was in the carriage, just as we reached the trainer's house, that the immense significance of the curried mutton occurred to me. You may remember that I was distrait, and remained sitting after you had all alighted. I was marvelling in my own mind how I could possibly have overlooked so obvious a clue."

"I confess," said the

Colonel, "that even now I cannot see how it helps us."

"It was the first link in my chain of reasoning. Powdered opium is by no means tasteless. The flavour is not disagreeable, but it is perceptible. Were it mixed with any ordinary dish the eater would undoubtedly detect it, and would probably eat no more. A curry was exactly the medium which would disguise this taste. By no possible supposition could this stranger, Fitzroy Simpson, have caused curry to be served in the trainer's family that night, and it is surely too monstrous a coincidence to suppose that he happened to come

along with powdered
opium upon the
very night when a
dish happened to be
served which would
disguise the flavour.
That is unthinkable.
Therefore Simpson
becomes eliminated
from the case, and
our attention centres
upon Straker and his
wife, the only two
people who could
have chosen curried
mutton for supper

that night. The opium was added after the dish was set aside for the stable-boy, for the others had the same for supper with no ill effects. Which of them, then, had access to that dish without the maid seeing them?

"Before deciding that question I had grasped the significance of the silence of the dog, for one true inference invariably suggests others. The Simpson incident had shown me that a dog was kept in the stables, and yet, though some one had been in and had fetched out a horse, he had not barked enough to arouse the two lads in the loft. Obviously the midnight visitor was some one whom the dog knew well.

"I was already convinced, or almost convinced, that John Straker went down to the stables in the dead of the night and took out Silver Blaze. For what purpose? For a dishonest one, obviously, or why should he drug his own stable-boy? And yet I was at a loss to know why. There have been cases before now where trainers have made sure of great sums of money by laying against their own horses, through agents, and then preventing them from winning by fraud. Sometimes it is a pulling jockey. Sometimes it is some surer and subtler means. What was it here? I hoped that the contents of his pockets might help me to form a conclusion.

"And they did so. You cannot have forgotten the singular knife which was found in the dead man's hand, a knife which certainly no sane man would choose for a weapon. It was, as Dr. Watson told us, a form of knife which is used for the most delicate operations known in surgery. And it was to be used for a delicate operation that night. You must know, with your wide experience of turf matters, Colonel Ross, that it is possible to make a slight nick upon the tendons of a horse's ham, and to do it subcutaneously, so as to leave absolutely no trace. A horse so treated would develop a slight lameness, which would be put down to a strain in exercise or a touch of rheumatism, but never to foul play."

"Villain! Scoundrel!" cried the Colonel.

"We have here the explanation of why

John Straker wished
to take the horse out
on to the moor. So
spirited a creature
would have certainly
roused the soundest
of sleepers when
it felt the prick of
the knife. It was
absolutely necessary
to do it in the open
air."

"I have been blind!"
cried the Colonel.
"Of course that was

why he needed the candle, and struck the match."

"Undoubtedly. But in examining his belongings I was fortunate enough to discover not only the method of the crime, but even its motives. As a man of the world, Colonel, you know that men do not carry other people's bills about

in their pockets.
We have most of us
quite enough to do
to settle our own. I
at once concluded
that Straker was
leading a double life,
and keeping a second
establishment. The
nature of the bill
showed that there
was a lady in the
case, and one who
had expensive
tastes. Liberal as
you are with your

servants, one can hardly expect that they can buy twenty-guinea walking dresses for their ladies. I questioned Mrs. Straker as to the dress without her knowing it, and having satisfied myself that it had never reached her, I made a note of the milliner's address, and felt that by calling there with

Straker's photograph I could easily dispose of the mythical Derbyshire.

"From that time on all was plain. Straker had led out the horse to a hollow where his light would be invisible. Simpson in his flight had dropped his cravat, and Straker had picked it up—with some idea, perhaps, that he might use it in securing the horse's leg. Once in the hollow, he had got behind the horse and had struck a light; but the creature frightened at the sudden glare, and with the strange instinct of animals feeling that some mischief was intended, had lashed out, and the steel shoe had struck

Straker full on the forehead. He had already, in spite of the rain, taken off his overcoat in order to do his delicate task, and so, as he fell, his knife gashed his thigh. Do I make it clear?"

"Wonderful!" cried the Colonel. "Wonderful! You might have been there!"

"My final shot was, I confess a very long one. It struck me that so astute a man as Straker would not undertake this delicate tendon-nicking without a little practice. What could he practice on? My eyes fell upon the sheep, and I asked a question which, rather to my surprise, showed that my surmise was correct.

"When I returned to London I called upon the milliner, who had recognised Straker as an excellent customer of the name of Derbyshire, who had a very dashing wife, with a strong partiality for expensive dresses. I have no doubt that this woman had plunged him over head and ears in debt, and so led him into this miserable plot."

"You have explained all but one thing," cried the Colonel. "Where was the horse?"

"Ah, it bolted, and was cared for by one of your neighbours. We must have an amnesty in that direction, I think. This is Clapham Junction, if I am not mistaken, and we shall be in Victoria in less than ten minutes. If you care to smoke a cigar in our rooms, Colonel, I shall be happy to give you any other details which might interest you."

THE END

ABOUT THE AUTHOR

Sir Arthur Conan Doyle was a British writer. Originally a physician, he struggled to find a publisher for his work at first. He modelled Sherlock Holmes on his former university teacher Joseph Bell. His Holmes stories are generally considered milestones in the field of crime fiction.

ABOUT THE COVER

The image on the cover is adapted from a silhouette of Basil Rathbone as Sherlock Holmes by Rumensz.

WHAT WE'RE ABOUT

I started making Super Large Print books for my grandma. I wanted books that she could keep reading as her glaucoma and macular degeneration advanced. So I chose a font originally designed for people with dyslexia, because the letters are bold and easy to distinguish. It is set at 30 pt, nearly twice the size of traditional Large Print books.

Digital reading was too frustrating for my grandma. It could never offer the pleasures she had always associated with reading: the peacefulness of turning a page, the satisfaction in knowing a story has "this much left," and the comforting memories of adventure, companionship, and revelation she felt when seeing the cover of her favorite book. Part of what makes reading so relaxing and grounding is the tactile experience. I hope these books can bring joy to those who want to keep reading and to those who've never had the pleasure of curling up with a page turner.

Please let me know if these books are helpful to you and if you have any requests for new titles. To leave feedback and to see the complete and constantly updating catalog, please visit:

superlargeprint.com

MORE BOOKS AT:

superlargeprint.com

KEEP ON READING!

ISBN 9781688307988